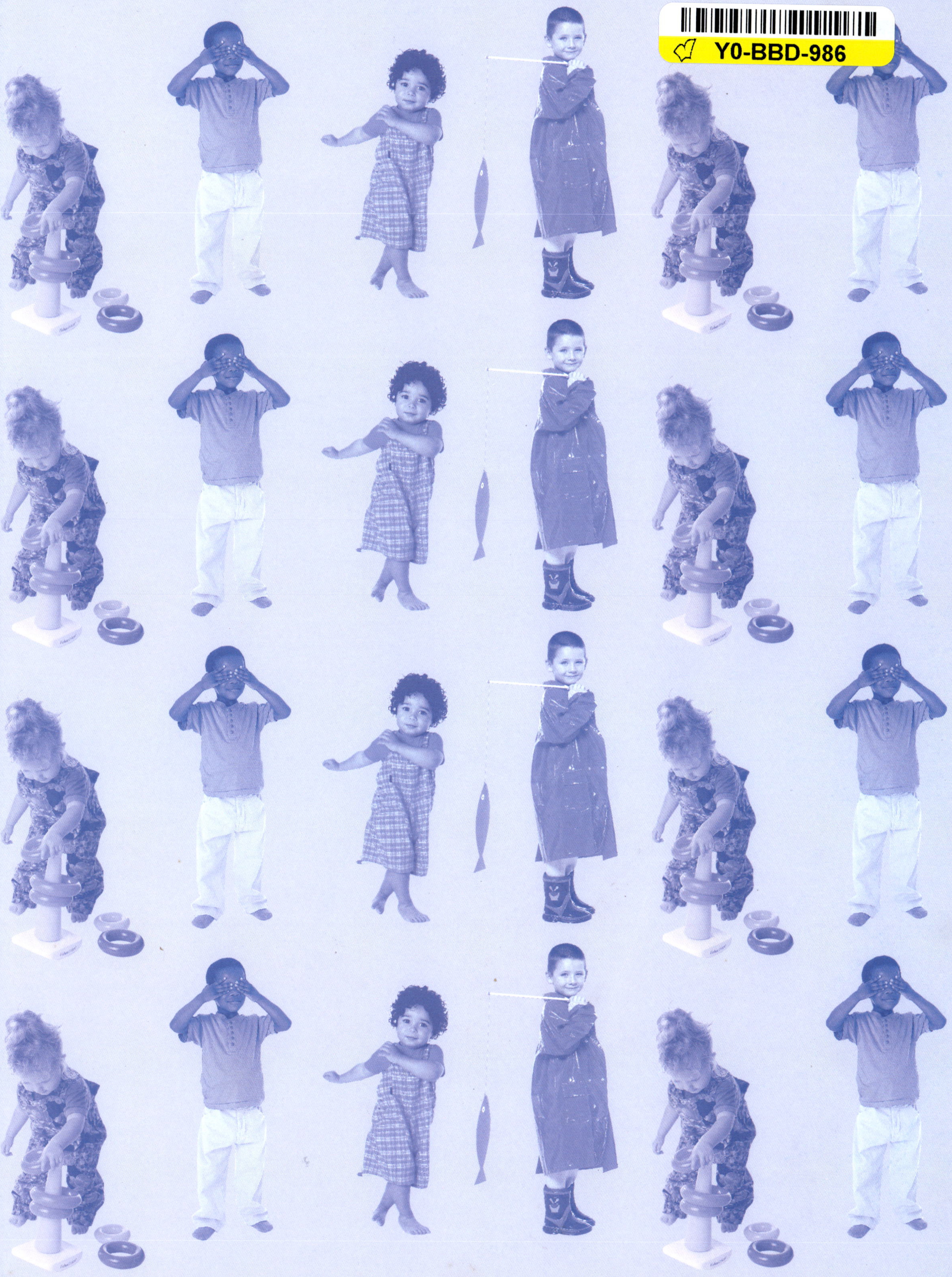

Having Fun

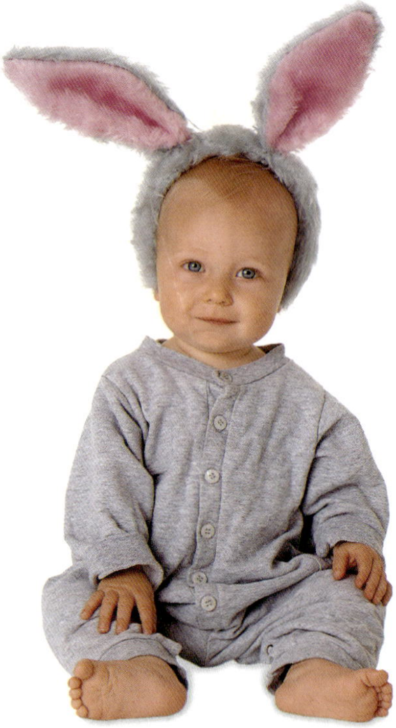
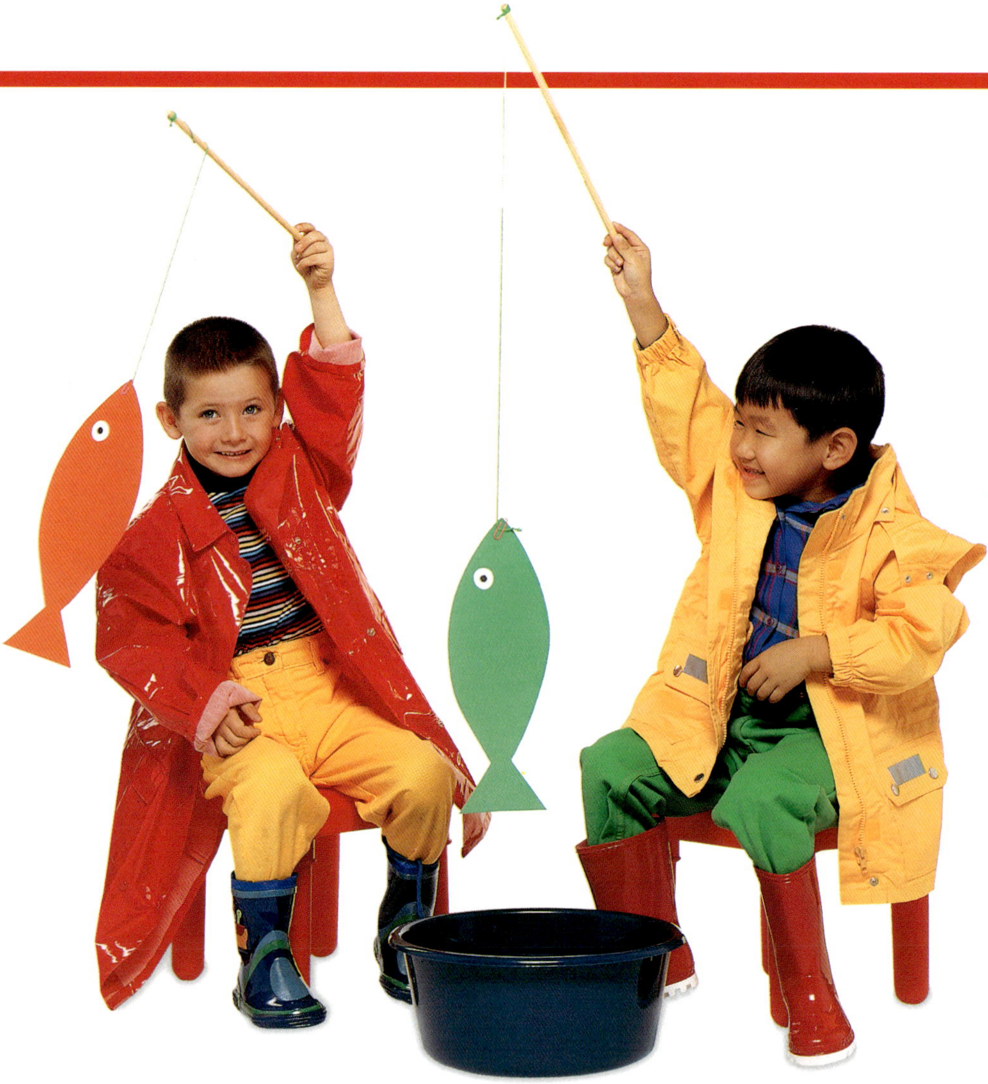
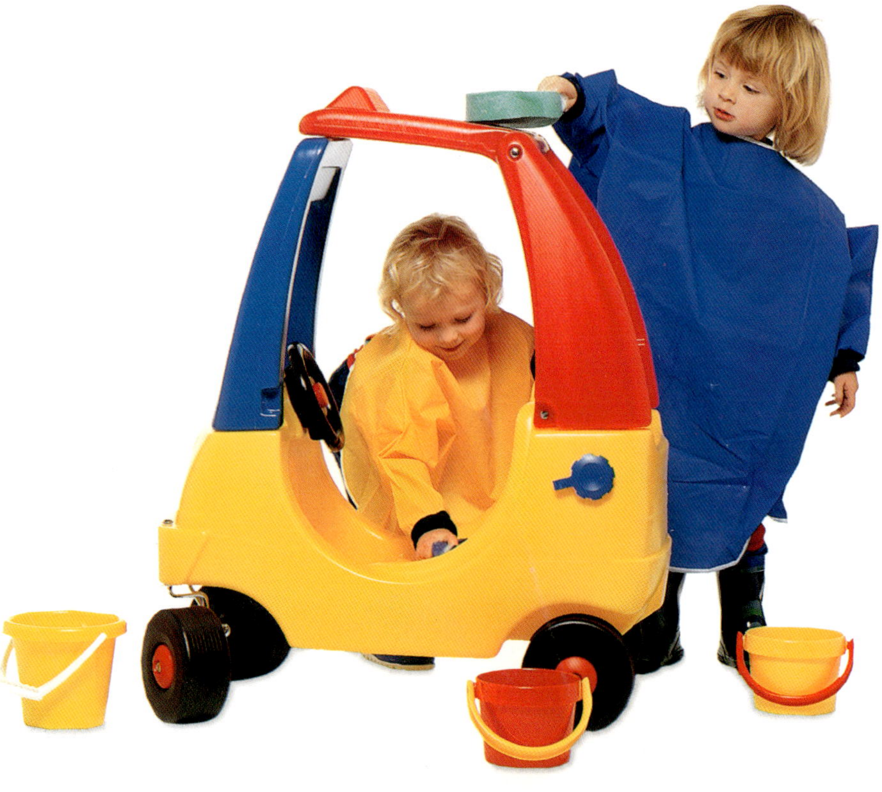
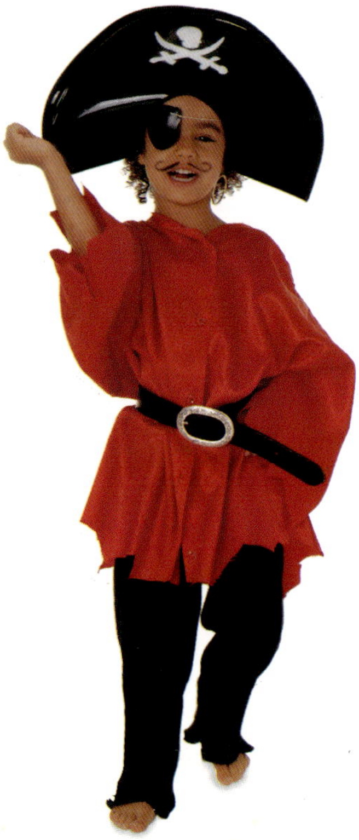

point and say

Having Fun
a very first picture book

HERMES HOUSE

First published in 1998 by Hermes House

Hermes House books are available for bulk purchase for sales promotion and for premium use.
For details write or call the sales director

Hermes House, 27 West 20th Street, New York, NY 10011
(800) 354-9657

© Anness Publishing Limited 1998

Hermes House is an imprint of Anness Publishing Inc.

All rights reserved. No part of this publication may be reproduced, stored in a retrieval system, or transmitted in any way or by any means, electronic, mechanical, photocopying, recording or otherwise, without the prior written permission of the copyright holder.

ISBN 1 84038 155 8

Publisher: Joanna Lorenz
Senior Editor: Catherine Barry
Designer: Simon Wilder

Printed in Hong Kong/China

1 3 5 7 9 10 8 6 4 2

Contents

Toys

Indoor Fun

Outdoor Fun

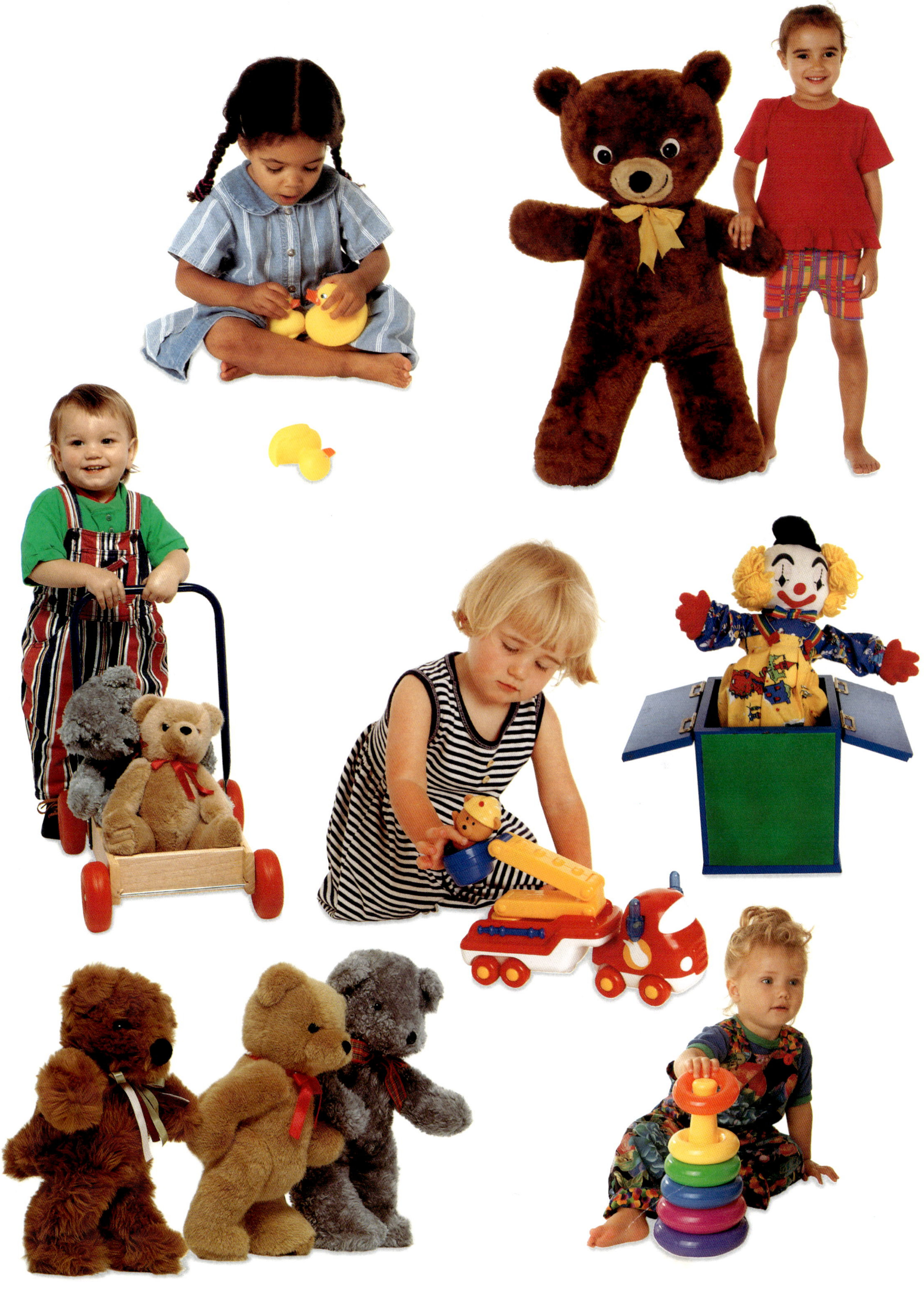

Toys

Bike

I'm riding my bike.

Catch me if you can.

I can go fast.

Look at me!

Teddy bears like to ride on bikes.

Rings

Where do these go?

That's it.

Ducks

We like
swimming in
the bathtub.

Say hello.

Quack, quack!

Rattle

Rattles make a loud noise.

Mmm – this rattle is tasty.

My rattle is fun!

Trumpet

I can blow a trumpet.

What a loud noise!

Fire Engine

Fire engines carry firefighters to a fire.

I've got to put
a fire out!

Almost there!
Wooo!
Wooo!

Help the firefighter
into the building.

Soft Toys

These are my furry friends.

duck

frog

snake

octopus

What's your name?

I'm called Pinkie.

Tow Truck

Tow trucks rescue cars and their passengers.

Have you broken down?

I will tow you to the garage.
Brrrm!
Brrrm!

Jack-in-the-Box

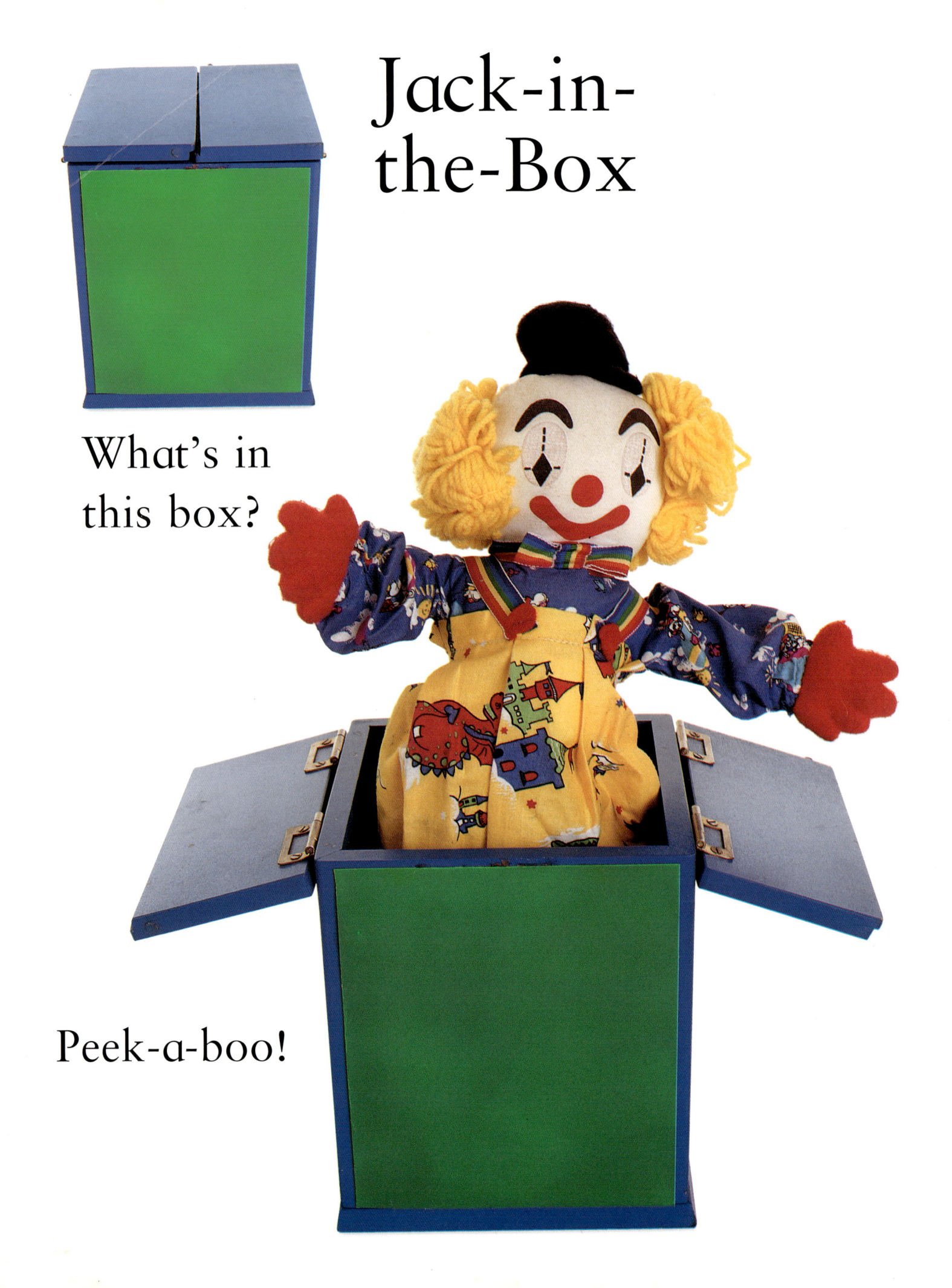

What's in this box?

Peek-a-boo!

Rag Doll

Hello.

Train

We are going on a long journey by train.

Choo, choo!

Can I come?

The train is speeding down the track.

Drum

We like banging on drums.

Bang! Bang! Bang!

What a loud noise. Rat-a-tat-tat!

Teddy Bears

Teddy bears are big...

or small.

They can be brown...

or gray...

or old.

Teddy bears like to go for walks...

or ride in a stroller.

They like to
ride on bikes...

or drive
in a car.

We are going
to the park.

Teddy bears like to play hide-and-seek.

I'll count to ten.

Where are you?

I can see you.

These teddy bears are in a band.

drum

tambourine

triangle

harmonica

What a noise!

Please stop playing!

Can you match the right toy

fire engine

bike

tow truck

rings

Jack-in-the-Box

teddy bear

drum

to the right words?

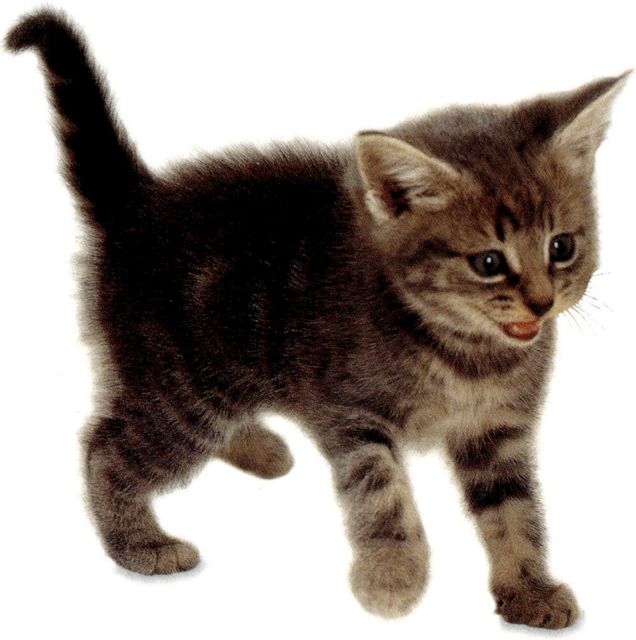
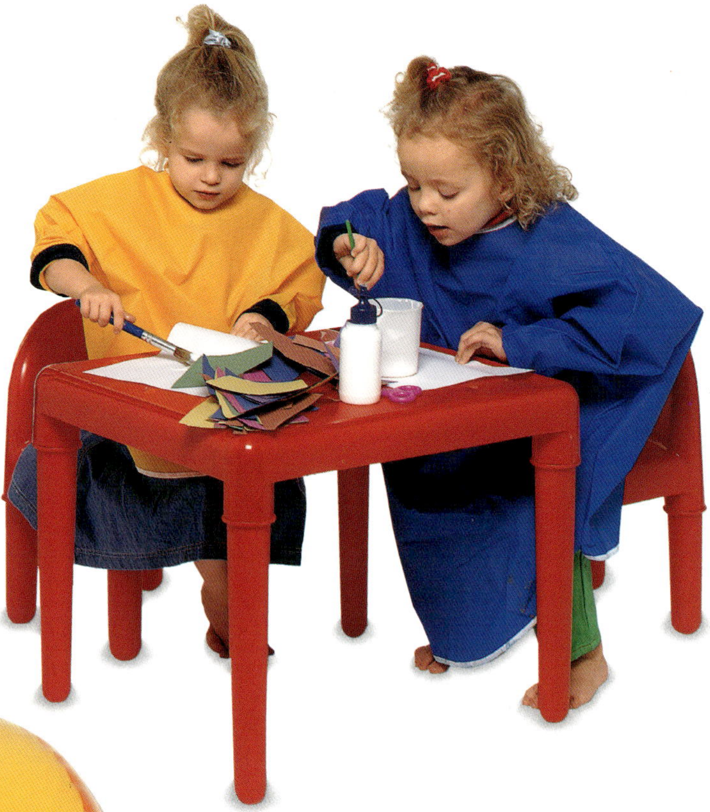
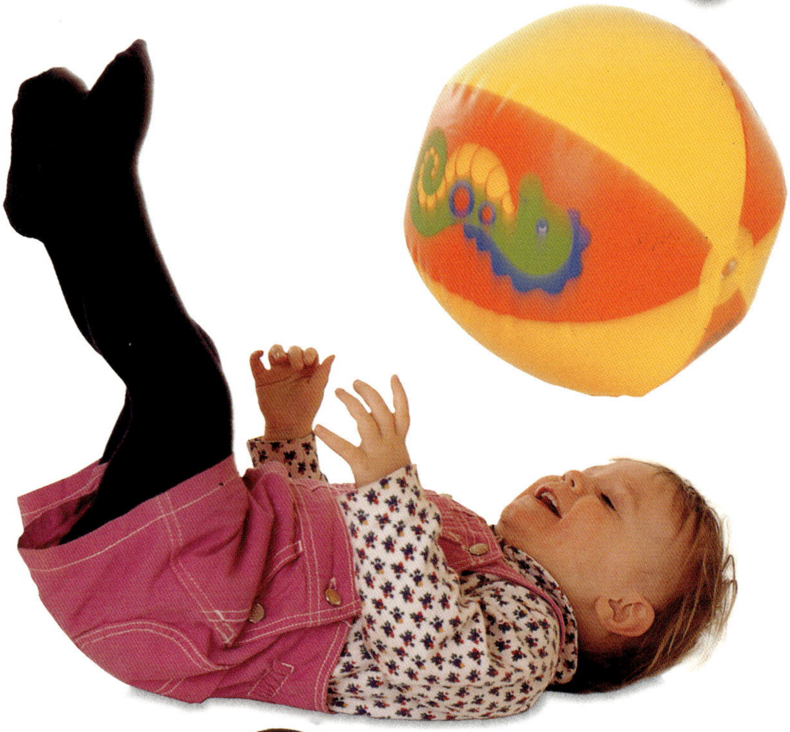
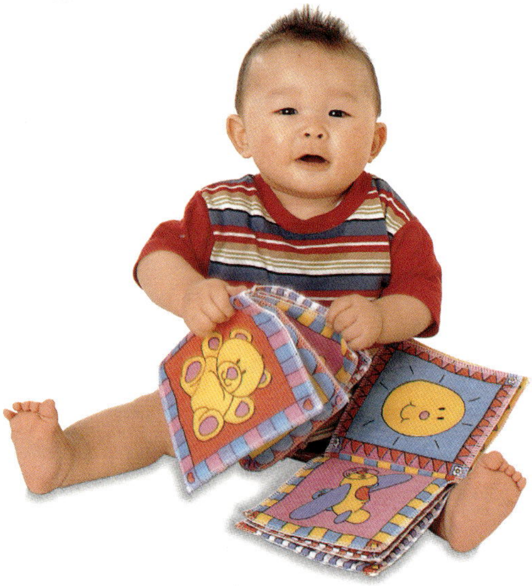
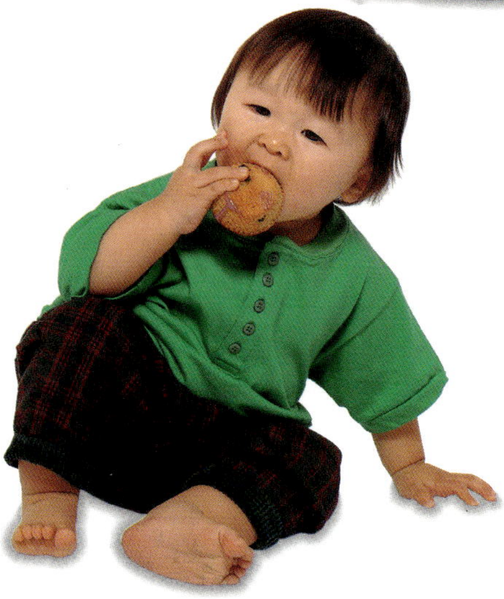
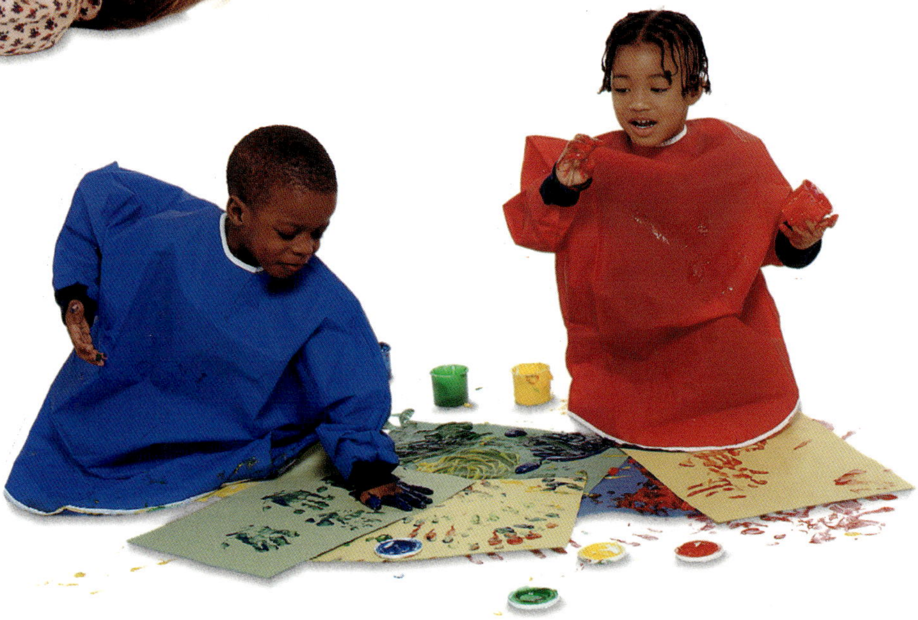

Indoor Fun

Dressing Up

I'm a ballerina.

I'm a magic wizard.

We're clowns.

I'm a sheriff today.

I'm a scary pirate.

And I'm a bunny rabbit.

Funny Faces

Grrrh!

I've got yellow cheeks.

We've got blue cheeks.

Look at my whiskers.

Look at my mustache.

Yum, yum!

Kittens

Who will play with me?

Kittens love to play with string.

What a mess!

They like to
play with a ball.

Kittens like
to be
petted.

Hello.

Painting

We are painting.

Do you like my pictures?

I've made a mess.

paints

brushes

We are painting with our hands...

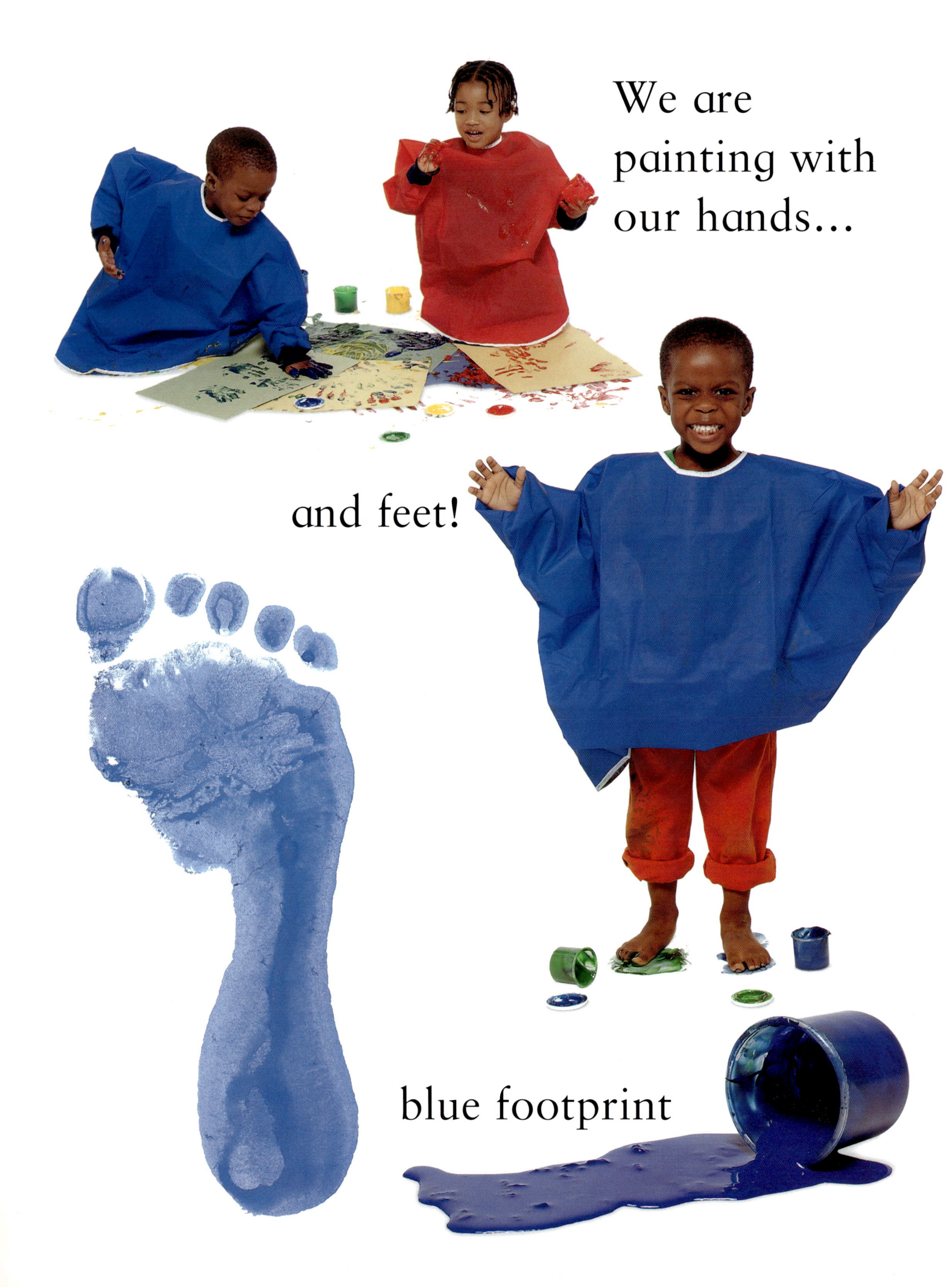

and feet!

blue footprint

green footprint

This is my favorite painting.

Dancing

We are dancing.

Turn the music up.

Balls

Should I throw now?

Catch!

This ball is bouncy.

Look at me!

I can roll my ball.

Building Blocks

Look at all these colors.

I'm building a wall.

wall of building blocks

I'm building a tower.

Look out!

Oops... I've knocked the wall over.

Playhouse

Welcome to our house.

Here's the window.

Here's the door.

Who's inside the house?

Hello!

Making a Collage

Making a collage is very messy.

The paper has stuck to my hand!

Who is going to clean up?

I'll help.

Making Cupcakes

We're making cupcakes.

Let's taste the frosting.

I'm putting the batter into the cupcake tins.

Do you want some frosting?

Yum. Cupcakes taste good.

Books

What are these books about?

This looks good.

It's a story book.

Will you read me a story?

Teddy is listening, too.

Toys

We are playing with toys.

dump truck

cement mixer

backhoe

lamb

chicken

tractor

car

cow

Can you match the right words

reading

dressing up

face painting

collage

playing with a ball

to the right pictures?

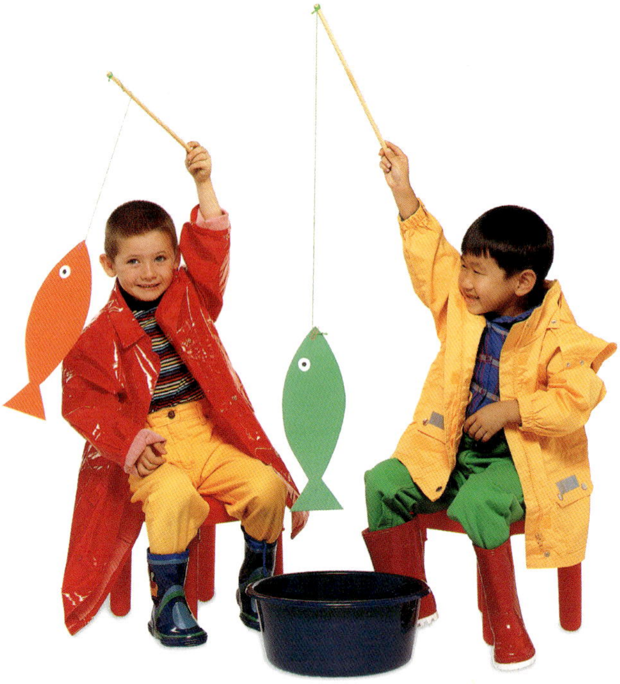
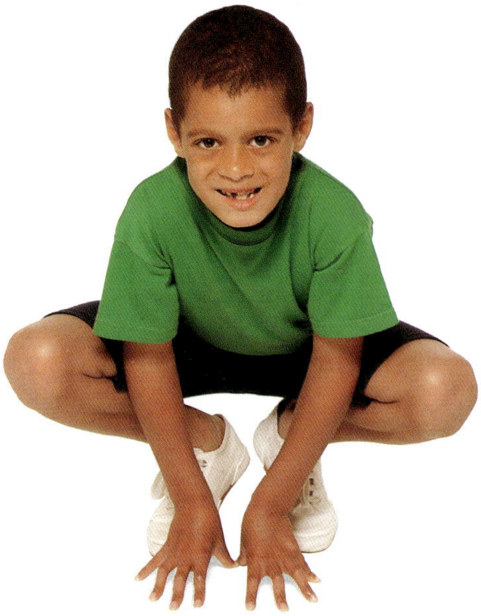
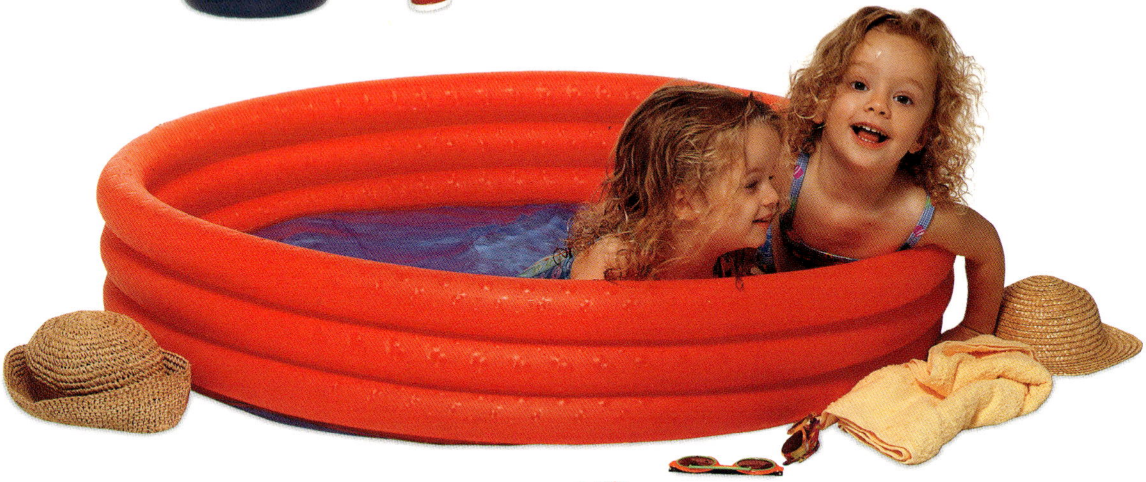
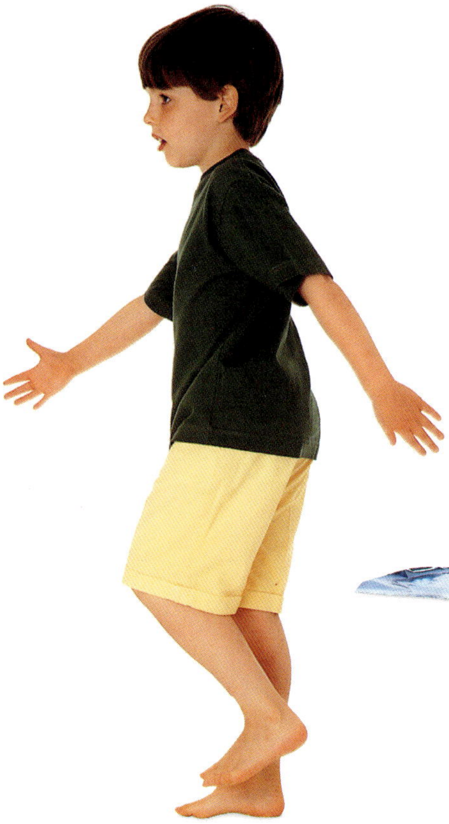
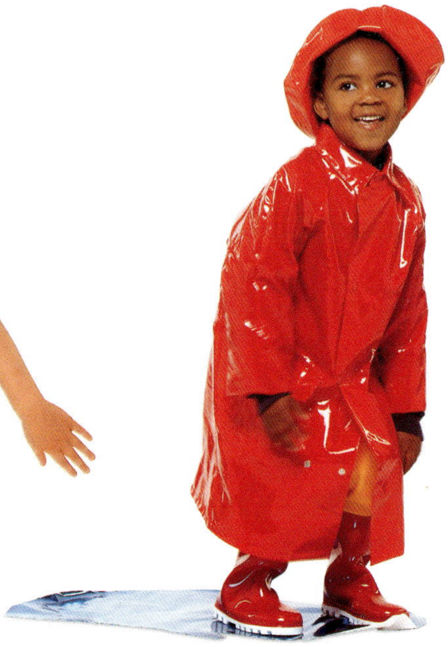
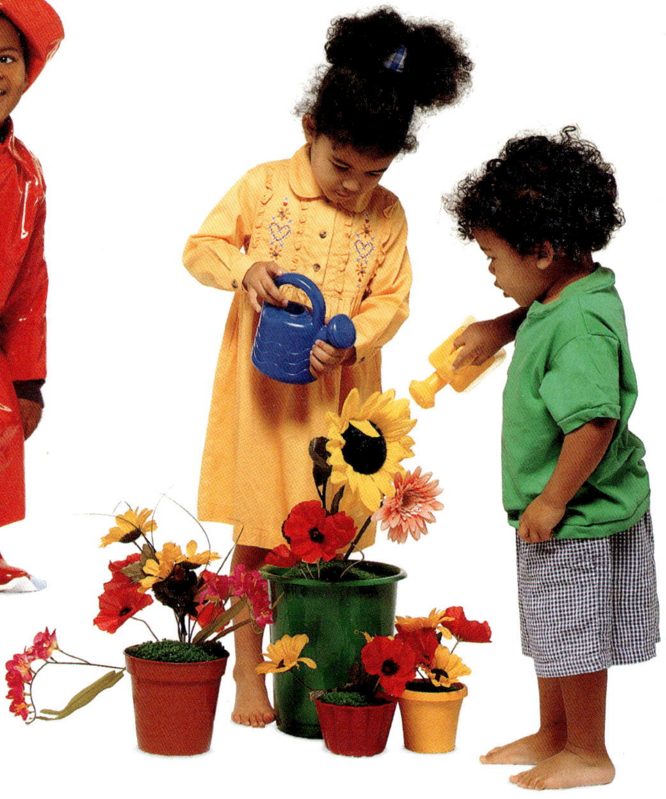

Outdoor Fun

Hopping

You hop on one leg.

Let's have a hopping race.

Ouch, you hopped on my foot!

Can you hop?

Skipping

We can skip around the playground.

We are jumping with a rope.

Can you jump rope?

Jumping

We can jump up...

...and down.

How high can you jump?

I can jump over these blocks.

I can jump over this sandcastle.

Running

We are running.

That's my cap! Stop!

I can run faster than you!

Marching

We are marching in a parade. Follow me!

I can walk like a giant...

and I can walk backward.

Hiding

We are playing hide-and-seek.

Here I come, ready or not!

I'm hiding behind the curtain.

Throwing

I can throw...

and I can catch.

I'm going to knock down all the pins.

Flying

We are flying high up in the air.

I'm an airplane.

I'm a bird.

Feeding the Ducks

We are going to feed the ducks.

You look hungry.

Ducks like to eat bread.

Walking the Dog

I am taking the dog for a walk.

We're ready to go.

He has a leash.

Come on!

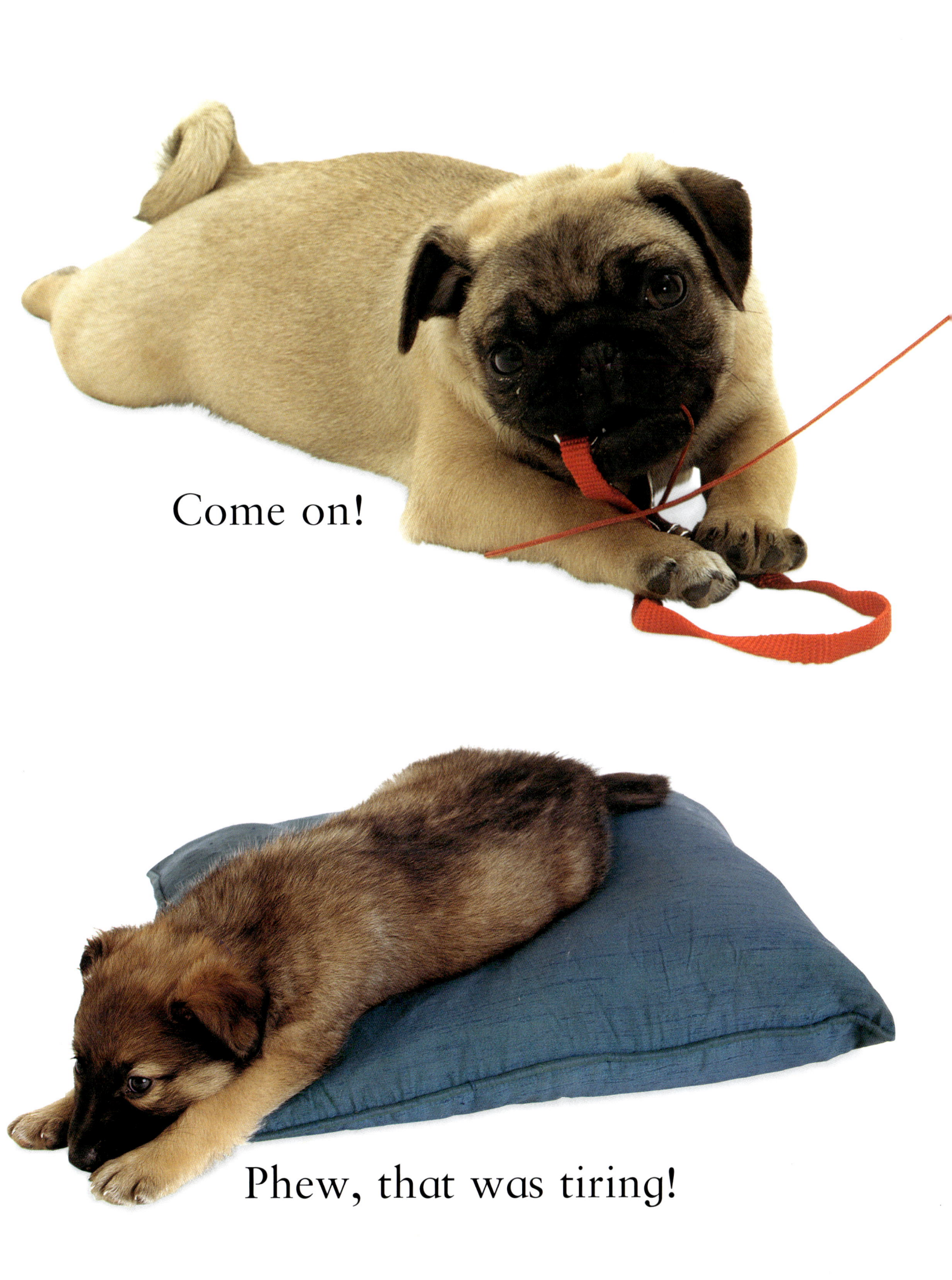

Phew, that was tiring!

Going Fishing

We are fishing.

Do you think we'll catch anything today?

Look! We both caught whoppers!

Let's take them home for supper.

Playing in the Rain

It's raining.

We are ready to play. We are wearing raincoats and boots.

Wheee! I'm jumping in a puddle.

I'm wet.

Whoops...

I'm sitting in a puddle.

Cleaning the Car

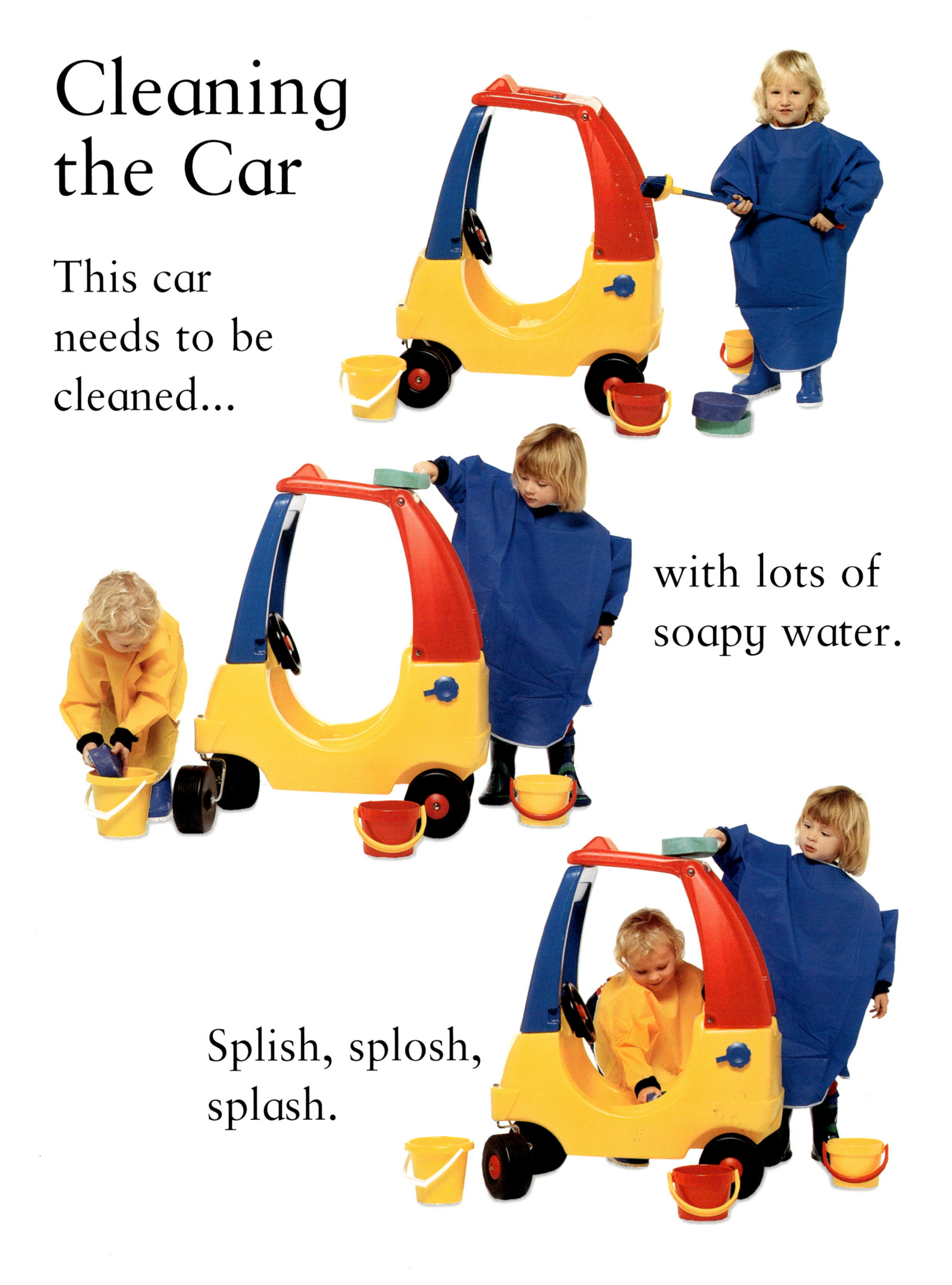

This car needs to be cleaned...

with lots of soapy water.

Splish, splosh, splash.

That looks fun.
Can I help?

liquid soap

sponge

Paddling

We're playing in the wading pool.

We like splashing the water.

We like splashing with our feet.

We're swimming.

The water feels cold.

I'd better dry off.

Gardening

We are going to water the flowers.

This flower needs lots of water.

flowers

fork

flowerpots

watering can

Can I help?

garden tools

Playing in the sandbox

We are building sandcastles.

spade

sandcastles

truck

buckets
of sand

Look at my nice,
round castle.

Oh no! it has
fallen down.

Can you match the right words

playing in the sandbox

paddling

skipping

fishing

jumping

to the right pictures?

Acknowledgments

The publishers would like to thank the following children for modeling for this series of books:

Rosie Anness, Daisy Bartel, Harriet Bartholomew, Jonathan Bartholomew, Chilli Bernstein, Caspian Broad, Karl Bolger, Lee Bolger, April Cain, Milo Clare, Tayah Ettienne, Matthew Ferguson, Africa George, Safari George, Saffron George, Jamie Grant, Faye Harrison, Zoe Harrison, Jack Harvey-Holt, Max Harvey-Holt, Erin Hoel, Alice Jenkins, Kathleen Jenkins, Becky Johnson, Zamour Johnson, Rebekah Murrell, Amber McLaren, Nell Nixon, Tiffani Ogilvie, Giovanni Sipiano, Guiseppe Sipiano and Ella Wilks-Harper.

All photographs © Anness Publishing Ltd.

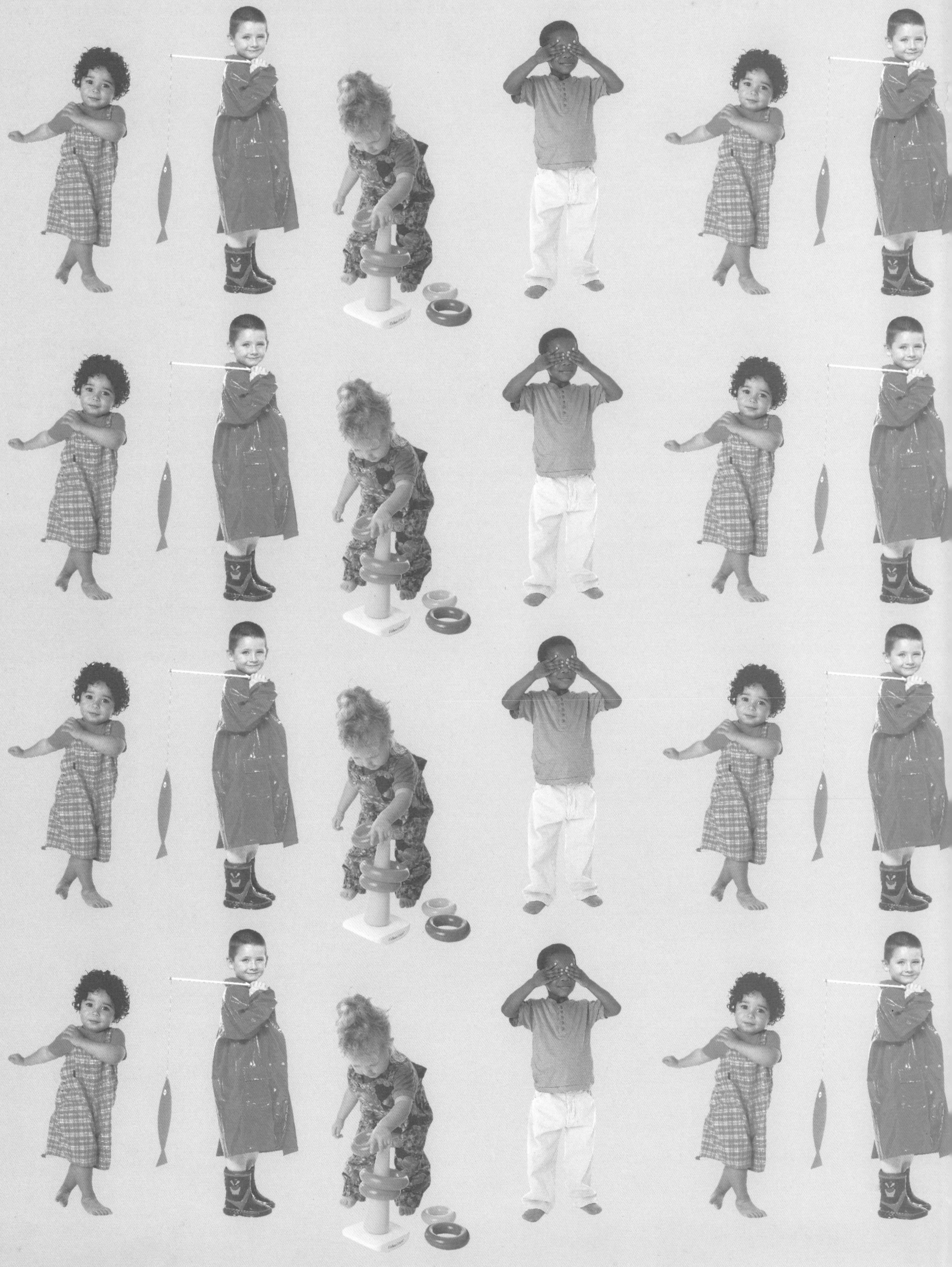